ELIZABETH

by Liesel Moak Skorpen
Pictures by Martha Alexander

SAN MATEO COUNTY LIBRARY SYSTEM
BELMONT, CALIFORNIA

Harper & Row, Publishers
New York, Evanston, and London

COPY 16

ELIZABETH

Text copyright © 1970 by Liesel Moak Skorpen
Pictures copyright © 1970 by Martha Alexander

All rights reserved. No part of this book may be used or repro-
duced in any manner whatsoever without written permission except in the case of brief quotations embodied in critical articles
and reviews. Printed in the United States of America. For informa-
tion address Harper & Row, Publishers, Inc., 49 East 33rd Street,
New York, N.Y. 10016. Published simultaneously in Canada by
Fitzhenry & Whiteside Limited, Toronto.

Library of Congress Catalog Card Number: 76-105490
7071727387654321

For Kate of course

"What do you want for Christmas?" asked Kate's mother.

"I want a red ball," said Kate, "and a new dress and a book and a doll. I want a doll with golden curls who walks and talks and turns somersaults."

"Well," said Kate's mother, "we shall see what surprises Christmas brings."

5

It seemed as though Christmas would never come, but of course Christmas came. Kate opened her presents under the tree. There was a red ball and a new dress and a book and other gifts. And underneath them all, in a long white box, there was a doll. It was a soft cloth doll with warm brown eyes and thick brown braids like Kate's.

"What does it do?" asked Kate.

"Everything a doll's supposed to do," her mother said.

Kate picked the doll up from its box. Its arms hung limply at its sides. Its weak legs flopped, and they couldn't hold it up. "What's its name?" asked Kate.

"She doesn't have a name," Kate's mother said. "No one has a name until somebody loves her."

Kate set the doll back in the box. "Thank you," she said to her mother politely. "It's an ugly doll," she said to herself inside. "It's an ugly doll, and I hate it very much."

There were no more presents under the tree.

Kate's cousin Agnes came for Christmas dinner. Agnes had a new doll whose name was Charlotte Louise. Charlotte Louise could walk and talk. "Where is your Christmas doll?" asked Agnes.

Kate showed her the cloth doll lying in the box.

"What does it do?" asked Agnes.

"It doesn't do anything," Kate replied.

"What is its name?" asked Agnes.

"It doesn't have a name," said Kate.

"It certainly is an ugly doll," said Agnes. She set Charlotte Louise down on the floor, and Charlotte Louise turned a somersault.

"I hate you, Agnes," Kate said, "and I hate your ugly doll!"

Kate was sent upstairs to bed without any pumpkin pie.

The next day was the day after Christmas. Kate's mother asked her to put away her presents. Kate put away her red ball and her new dress and her book and all her other gifts except the doll.

"I don't want this ugly doll," she said to James the collie. "You may have it if you like."

James wagged his tail. He took the cloth doll in his mouth and carried it out to the snowy garden.

By lunchtime James hadn't come home, and Kate was sorry she had given her doll to him. She couldn't eat her sandwich or her cake. "James will chew that doll right up," she said to herself. "He'll chew and chew until there's nothing left but stuffing and some rags. He'll bury her somewhere in the snow."

She put on her coat and mittens and boots and went out into the garden. James was no-where to be seen. "I'm sorry," said Kate inside herself. "I'm very, very sorry, and I want to find my doll."

Kate looked all over the garden before she found her. The doll was lying under the cherry tree, half-buried in the snow, but except for being wet and cold, she seemed as good as new. Kate brushed her clean and cradled her in her arms. "It's all right now, Elizabeth," she said, "because I love you after all."

Elizabeth could do everything.
When Kate was happy, Elizabeth was happy.
When Kate was sad, Elizabeth understood.
When Kate was mad and said something mean and had to go upstairs, Elizabeth went with her.

16

Elizabeth didn't care for baths. "She doesn't like water," Kate explained, "because of being buried in the snow." Elizabeth sat on the edge of the tub and kept Kate company while she scrubbed.

Elizabeth loved to swing and slide and go around and around on the merry-go-round.

When Kate wanted to be the mother, Elizabeth was the baby.

When Kate wanted to be Cinderella, Elizabeth was a wicked stepsister and the fairy godmother too.

Sometimes Kate forgot about Elizabeth because she was playing with other friends.

Elizabeth waited patiently. When Kate came back, Elizabeth was always glad to see her.

In the spring, Elizabeth and Kate picked violets for Kate's mother's birthday and helped Kate's father fly a kite.

In the summer, everyone went to the seashore. Agnes was there too, but Agnes's doll, Charlotte Louise, was not.

"Where is Charlotte Louise?" Kate asked, holding Elizabeth in her arms.

"Charlotte Louise is broken," Agnes said. "We threw her in the trash. I shall have a new doll for Christmas."

Agnes wouldn't go into the water. She was afraid. But Kate went in for a dip. She set Elizabeth on a towel to sleep safely in the sun. When she came out of the water, Elizabeth was gone.

"Help," cried Kate, "please, somebody help! Elizabeth is drowning!"

Everyone heard the word "drowning," but nobody quite heard who. Grown-ups shouted and ran around pointing their fingers toward the sea.

Then out of nowhere
Like a streak,
Galloping, galloping,
James the collie came.

Out into the sea and back to shore he swam,
Elizabeth hanging limply from his mouth.

24

After an hour in the sun, Elizabeth was as good as new.

Everyone except Agnes said that James was brave and good and a hero.

Kate didn't say that Agnes had thrown Elizabeth into the sea, but inside herself she thought that Agnes had.

In the autumn, Elizabeth helped Kate gather berries in the meadow for jams and jellies and berry pies.

Then Christmas came again. Of course there were presents under the tree. For Kate, there was a new sled and a new dress and a book and other gifts. For Elizabeth, there was a woolen coat and hat, and two dresses, one of them velvet.

Agnes came for Christmas dinner. Agnes had a new doll whose name was Tina Marie.

"Tina Marie can sing songs," said Agnes. "She can blow bubbles too, and crawl along the floor."

Kate held Elizabeth tightly in her arms. "Well," said Kate in a whisper, "Tina Marie is the ugliest doll I ever saw. She is almost as ugly as you."

Agnes kicked Kate sharply on the leg and said the most dreadful things to Elizabeth, who was looking particularly well in her velvet dress.

Agnes's mother was very cross with Agnes.

Agnes spent the rest of the day in disgrace and wasn't permitted any pumpkin pie.

"Merry Christmas, Elizabeth," said Kate as
she tucked her into bed, "and Happy Birthday
too! You are the best and most beautiful doll in
the world, and I wouldn't trade you for any-
one else."